# The Wrong Bus

# LOIS PETERSON

# The Wrong Bus

illustrated by
## AMY
## MEISSNER

ORCA BOOK PUBLISHERS

**Library and Archives Canada Cataloguing in Publication**

Peterson, Lois J., 1952-
The wrong bus / Lois Peterson ; illustrated by Amy Meissner.
(Orca echoes)

Issued also in electronic formats.
ISBN 978-1-55469-869-1

I. Meissner, Amy  II. Title.  III. Series: Orca echoes
PS8631.E832W76 2012      JC813'.6      C2011-907535-0

First published in the United States, 2012
**Library of Congress Control Number**: 2011942582

Summary: When Jack's grandpa dies, Jack boards the wrong bus, which turns out to be the right
bus to say goodbye to his beloved grandfather.

Orca Book Publishers gratefully acknowledges the support for its publishing programs
provided by the following agencies: the Government of Canada through the Canada Book
Fund and the Canada Council for the Arts, and the Province of British Columbia
through the BC Arts Council and the Book Publishing Tax Credit.

 MIX
Paper from
responsible sources
FSC
www.fsc.org  FSC® C004071

 ANCIENT FOREST ™
FRIENDLY

*Orca Book Publishers is dedicated to preserving the environment and has printed this book
on paper certified by the Forest Stewardship Council®.*

10% of author royalties will be donated to Volunteer Grandparents (Vancouver)

Cover artwork and interior illustrations by Amy Meissner
Author photo by E. Henry

ORCA BOOK PUBLISHERS
PO Box 5626, Stn. B
Victoria, BC Canada
V8R 6S4

ORCA BOOK PUBLISHERS
PO Box 468
Custer, WA USA
98240-0468

www.orcabook.com
Printed and bound in Canada.

15  14  13  12  •  4  3  2  1

*For my grandsons, Copper Johnston and Colton Brunt.*
*In memory of my own grandfather,*
*Joseph Lemmon, who worked "on the buses." —LP*


*Many thanks to the crew of the Arctic Passage —ACM*

# Chapter One

Mom wouldn't let Jack go to Grandpa Nod's funeral. "Eight-year-olds don't belong at cemeteries," she said.

But she did let him take the day off school. She left him with a word-puzzle book, two new green felt pens (his favorite kind) and a handful of fruit strips. "I'll be back at three," she said. "Mrs. Barrett will stay with you until I get back."

Jack waited for his mom to lock the door. Then he looked out the window and watched her go.

Soon the Number 26 bus came along. Mom got on. He waved, but no one waved back.

Jack watched seven buses go past before Mom came home. Her eyes were red. She was carrying

a white daisy. She put it in a skinny vase on the table. When she took off her coat, a bundle of tissues fell out of her coat pocket.

"You didn't even open that book," she said. "I thought apple strips were your favorite."

Jack couldn't tell her he had been waiting for Grandpa's bus. If he did, she would tell him he should stop waiting. Grandpa Nod was gone. He couldn't come back, even if he wanted to.

Jack didn't tell her he wished he had said goodbye.

"Hospitals are not for eight-year-olds," she had told him more than once. Just like funeral homes and cemeteries weren't either.

# Chapter Two

"School today, as usual. Off you go," Mom said the next morning.

Katy Doyle, from the upstairs apartment, was in Jack's class. She waited for the bus with him, as usual. So did Leah from the third floor. Today Leah's tights were black and white squares. They reminded Jack of a checkerboard.

"When I grow up, I'm going to buy my clothes where Leah does," said Katy, as usual.

As usual, Leah didn't look at Jack or Katy. She just cracked her gum and stared at the sidewalk.

Jack didn't mind. He knew teenagers only had time for eight-year-olds when they babysat them.

Jack let Katy and Leah on the bus first. Then he let on the lady who carried her dog in a basket.

"Let's get this show on the road," said the bus driver.

"Come on, Jack," said Katy. She waited for him on the top step.

"This is my grandpa's bus," said Jack.

"I bet you're Jack. Noddy's grandson," said the driver. "He told us all about you."

"This is my grandpa's bus," Jack said again.

"He died," Katy told the driver in her helpful voice.

"I'm sorry about your grandpa," said the driver. His voice was kind. But his hand was on the knob that closed the door. "Hop aboard now. Let's get this show on the road."

"Come on, Jack," said Katy.

Jack picked up his backpack and climbed on the bus.

Today, instead of sitting beside Katy, he sat behind her. He pressed his face against the window and watched the streets swim by.

Mr. Singh was sweeping the sidewalk outside his shop. He swept it every morning. A man carrying a briefcase and a tennis racket boarded the bus at the Rec Center. He caught the bus every day. A teenager with a skateboard and lots of tattoos loped up the stairs. He boarded like that every morning.

Everything was the same as usual.

Except Grandpa Nod was not driving.

If Jack's grandpa had been driving bus Number 26, he would have said something special to everyone who got on. And he would have called Jack a candy name. Something like Double Bubble. Maybe Sen-Sen. Or perhaps his favorite—Jawbreaker.

This driver only grunted, "Hello." Or said, "Let's get this show on the road," if people took too long.

Jack and Katy got off the bus at school. Instead of saying, "See you later, Jelly Bean," the driver didn't say anything. He waited until Jack and Katy were safely down the steps. Then he closed the doors and drove away.

"Who's going to meet you after school now that your grandpa's dead?" Katy asked as they walked into school.

"I have to catch the bus home with you," Jack said.

"Cool. How about you sit beside me this time?"

Instead of taking the bus home with Katy, Jack would rather have his grandpa meet him. When Grandpa Nod picked him up, he always checked if Jack had eaten his sandwich, apple and carrot sticks. Then he ate whatever was left as they headed to the park, the bird sanctuary or the river to watch the tugboats.

Sometimes they took the bus. Grandpa had a bus pass, so he could get on for free. He knew all the drivers. When Jack was with him, the drivers let Jack on the bus for free too.

But usually they walked. And Grandpa Nod would sing.

Jack walked into class. "Glad to see you back," said Mr. Haworth.

"Jack's grandpa died," Katy helpfully told everyone.

Jack went to his desk. He put his lunchbox inside it and waited for roll call.

# Chapter Three

After school Katy said, "I just remembered. I have to stay and practice for the concert."

"You should have told me," Jack said. "Mom says eight-year-olds are too young to ride the bus alone."

"You won't be alone, silly. It will be full of people. It always is after school."

Jack waited and waited for the Number 26 bus. The Number 13 passed. Then the Number 17.

Maybe he could walk, he thought. His grandpa often walked him home from school. Jack knew the way.

There was no number on the next bus. Jack stepped back. He expected it to pass by, headed for the depot. But it stopped in front of him.

The doors wheezed open.

The sun shone in Jack's face. He couldn't see the driver.

"Hop on, son," a voice said.

"This is the wrong bus," Jack said. "I need the Number 26."

"This will do. Hop on, Jawbreaker."

Jawbreaker! Jack raced up the stairs. "Grandpa!"

The doors wheezed shut behind him.

"Who else?"

"Mom said you died."

"I did. But here I am. What a lark!"

Jack didn't know what to do. His grandpa had got sick. He was checked into the hospital. The hospital that was no place for an eight-year-old. So Jack hadn't been able to visit him. Then his grandpa died. His body went to the funeral home. The funeral home that was no place for an eight-year-old. Then Jack's mom left him at home while she

went to the cemetery. The cemetery that was also no place for an eight-year-old.

But here was Grandpa Nod!

"You'd better sit down," his grandpa said. "You look a bit shaky. And we're in for a heck of a ride."

"Where are we going?" asked Jack.

"Here, there and everywhere in between. A Magical Mystery Tour."

Jack grinned. It was just the kind of thing his grandpa always said. "Where are the other passengers?" he asked.

"They can get the next bus." Grandpa Nod chuckled. "As you said, this is the wrong bus. For everyone but the two of us." He put the bus in gear. "Sit down. It's time to make a break for it."

Jack sat on the long seat. He could watch his grandpa from there. He wrapped his hands tight around the silver pole.

The bus went through the intersection instead of turning right. "You're going the wrong way," Jack said.

"It's the wrong bus. Of course it's going the wrong way. Did you eat your lunch?" Grandpa asked.

"I wasn't hungry."

"Good-oh!" said Grandpa. "All the more for me."

Grandpa Nod drove the bus past the park. He turned onto a side street.

"You're going the wrong way," Jack said. "The sign says *One Way Only*."

"My bus doesn't care about signs," said Grandpa.

He stopped beside a very tall building.

*Emergency Department* was written across the big windows. "It says *No Parking*," said Jack. "Why are we here?"

Grandpa turned the engine off. He stood up. "Come on, Tic Tac. Let's go walkabout."

Jack held his grandfather's hand. It was cool as a breeze and light as a feather.

They left the bus on the yellow line and walked through the doors into the hospital.

The hall was long and narrow. People in white coats hurried in both directions.

Jack waited beside his grandfather in front of an elevator. "It says *Staff Only*," said Jack.

"It makes no nevermind to us," said Grandpa. The doors opened. Grandpa Nod winked at the lady on the gurney. Jack smiled at the porter holding an IV pole. But no one smiled back.

"Hit the button. We want the fifth floor," said Grandpa.

When they arrived, Jack and his grandfather waited until the gurney was rolled out. Jack didn't feel a thing as the wheels rolled over his feet. His grandfather didn't flinch when the porter bumped into him. "This-a-way," said Grandpa.

They walked down another long hallway. It was lined with trolleys, bins and medical equipment.

Grandpa pushed open the swinging doors that said *No Entry*. He led Jack past racks of blankets and carts loaded with bottles and basins. Everyone was too busy to notice them.

They stopped at Room 148.

Grandpa peered through a glass window in the middle of the door. He pushed the door open and stepped aside. "After you," he said to Jack.

# Chapter Four

The ward was dark and quiet. A door to the bathroom was open. But no one was inside.

One bed was empty and covered by a flat white sheet. The curtains were closed around the other bed. When Grandpa slid them open, the hooks rattled.

A man lay in the bed with his eyes closed. A blanket was pulled up to his neck.

"This was my bed," said Grandpa. Jack stared at the man. He looked at his grandfather.

"When your ma visited, I was a scary sight," said Grandpa. "Hooked up to all kinds of gizmos. Bells and whistles. Tubes here and there."

Jack held Grandpa Nod's hand. "Did it hurt?" he asked.

"A bit. Nothing I couldn't bear." Grandpa grinned. "The nurses were mighty nice," he said. A big man in a white jacket came into the room. A stethoscope hung around his neck. He twiddled with the machine above the sleeping patient's bed and went out again. "Even the big ugly ones like Ralph," said Grandpa.

"Who's Ralph?" asked Jack.

"That was Ralph," said Grandpa.

"Why did you die?" asked Jack. "Couldn't they fix you?"

"Too many bits were all worn out. Any minute they would start falling off." Grandpa patted the corner of the empty bed. "They did what they could. And I am much better now."

Jack looked across at the sleeping man. Maybe he had a grandson too. Maybe one who was younger than eight but was allowed to come and visit.

21

Jack walked around the room. He checked out the cards on the bedside table. He sniffed the limp flowers in the jug.

He stood over the man and watched him sleep.

Footsteps passed in the hall. Voices rose and fell. No one came in.

Grandpa Nod stood at the end of the man's bed, waiting for Jack to finish checking things out.

When Jack had finished his tour of the room, Grandpa Nod asked, "Seen enough?"

"Yes," said Jack. He took his grandfather's hand. It was cool and soft.

They walked back to the elevators. A nurse hurried toward them. Jack stepped aside so she wouldn't run into him. She walked past and kept going as if they weren't there.

They boarded the public elevator. A man studied a clipboard. A lady in a terry-towel housecoat and flip-flop slippers rode down with them. No one said a word.

Back at the bus, Jack checked the windshield. No parking ticket. "Don't you have to get back to your route?" he asked Grandpa.

"Not us. Places to go. People to see," he said. He drove through the intersection without stopping at the Stop sign.

# Chapter Five

Grandpa ran through three red lights and another Stop sign. He drove the wrong way up two one-way streets.

He ignored all the bus stops with people waiting in long lines.

No one honked at him. No police cars chased after them.

He pulled into a reserved parking spot at the Restful Haven Funeral Home. "Wanna come lookylook, Juicy Fruit?" he asked.

Jack walked past a long black limousine. Two ladies held on to each other's arms. Two men eased a casket into the back of the car.

Indoors, the lobby was shadowy and cool. Soft music played. A vase of flowers stood on a table. The scent filled the room like all kinds of mixed-up candy.

A man with a bald head and a dark suit ignored Jack and Grandpa as they walked toward the doors that said *Visitors Please Use Chapel Entrance.*

They entered a room filled with caskets. Some had half the lid wide open. Others were closed with little shiny plaques on top.

Jack stood close to his grandpa, holding his hand. He looked around. The lights were dim. A thick blue carpet covered the floor. Their footsteps did not make a sound as Jack's grandpa led him around the room.

"Which would you choose?" Grandpa asked.

One was shiny black all over, with silver studs along the edge of the lid. One was pure white and very small.

They all stood on high tables, so Jack couldn't see into the open ones. Most had big handles. Beside each casket was a sign with the price.

One cost $3,000. It sounded like a lot of money to Jack.

He walked to the back of the room. He laid his hand on a casket made of plain wood. It looked as if it had just come out of someone's workshop. It smelled of sharp-scented, fresh-cut wood. It had no fancy handles or gold plaques. Jack felt his grandpa watching him. "I like this one best," said Jack.

"You've got good taste, Life Saver," said Grandpa. "That's the one I would have picked." He stroked a dark brown casket. "But your ma wanted something fancier. As befitted the stature of the man inside."

"Was it dark in there?" asked Jack. "Could you breathe?"

"Didn't need to. It's all for show," said his grandpa. "But your ma was happy to see me tucked up tight."

Jack wondered if his grandpa wore his bus uniform and cap inside the casket. But he didn't ask.

"Seen enough?" asked Grandpa.

Jack looked around the room. It was so quiet and peaceful. He wouldn't mind taking a nap inside one of the coffins. But he didn't say so.

As they walked back out to the bus, people in dark suits and black dresses were headed in. No one moved to let them past. They skirted through the crowd without anyone saying anything to them.

"Where are we going now?" asked Jack.

Grandpa pulled away from the curb. He turned onto the street without stopping to check both ways first. "How can this be a Magical Mystery Tour if there's no mystery?" he said. "Stick with me, Milk Dud. You'll find out soon."

# Chapter Six

Jack had an idea where they were going. But he wasn't sure. He had never been to a cemetery.

Grandpa Nod drove along some streets Jack knew and some he didn't. They passed the grocery store where Mom shopped. They drove by the clinic where Jack once went to have a huge splinter removed. Jack peered out the front window and held on to the silver pole. He wondered where Grandpa Nod was taking him next.

His grandfather sang "The Wheels on the Bus." Jack thought eight-year-olds were too old for that song. But there was no one around to hear him hum along.

Jack had never been on an empty bus. He liked it. He felt like he was in a private world.

His grandpa drove through two more Stop signs and crossed over a bridge on the wrong side of the road. He drove through a crosswalk when a man with a boom box was walking in it. He made a left turn on Pine Street, even though it wasn't past six o'clock yet.

At last, Grandpa Nod pulled the bus into a handi-capped parking spot at the park. He set the brake and pushed the knob that opened the doors. "Coming?"

Jack and his mom often came to the Pine Valley Rec Center. They walked through the gardens and watched runners circle the track. Sometimes they went inside to watch people make pottery or play squash.

Today the water park was filled with babies splashing and toddlers running around with slappy footsteps. Mothers picked up towels and told children not to push.

Jack stopped at the sign that said *For Children Six and Under.*

His mom often said many things were not for eight-year-olds.

He was seven when they built the water park. He had always wanted to play there.

Jack checked to see if anyone who worked there was watching. But no one was looking their way.

"You coming or not?" asked Grandpa. "This might be your only chance." He was standing under a red spout. Water poured over his driver's cap and down his driver's uniform and into his shiny black driver's shoes.

Jack went down the waterslide twice. No one yelled at him when he bumped into a toddler who didn't seem to notice.

He and grandpa held hands and turned in circles. The sprinkler rained warm water down on them. None of the mothers told them to watch out for the babies.

Jack turned the wheel that made the water go on and off and on again. The little girl standing under the nozzle didn't complain.

They walked back to the bus. They were both dry before they got there. "I've always wanted to do that," said Jack.

"I figured as much, Licorice Whip," said Grandpa. He turned out of the parking lot the wrong way. "Just one more stop on my Magical Mystery Tour," he said.

# Chapter Seven

Grandpa ignored the young woman directing traffic near some road works. Even though the sign said *Traffic Fines Double in Construction Zones*. He didn't even slow down when a little dog ran onto the road in front of the bus.

Jack looked back. He was relieved to see the dog had arrived safely on the other side.

They drove up a big hill where they could look down over the town below them. Grandpa ignored the sign that said *Authorized Vehicles Only*. He followed a curving path to the very top.

When he turned off the engine, everything was very quiet. A bird flashed in front of the window. From far away came the sound of a lawn mower.

"Let's go walkabout," said Grandpa Nod.

They left the bus parked in the middle of the path. They stepped off the bus onto the grass. All around them were gravestones, statues and flowers. Some flowers were fresh and in vases. Others were faded and lying on the ground.

Jack shivered. "Is this where they buried you?" he asked.

"Sure is. Did you ever see such a peaceful spot?" said Grandpa. When he took Jack's hand in his it was cool as a breeze and soft as a feather.

He led Jack through the cemetery. They stopped to read the names on the headstones. They straightened a flower that had fallen out of its vase. They studied a statue of a smiling cherub.

They came to a small patch of ground under a tree. A shiny black slab of stone said:

*Selena Deacon 1952–2002*
*Loved and lost but never forgotten.*
*Beloved wife of Neil (Noddy) Deacon*

"That was my grandma, wasn't it?" asked Jack. He had heard lots about her. She had died before he was born.

"That she was," said Grandpa Nod. "She got here first. Always had a competitive streak, my Selena."

Next to his grandma's grave was a seam in the grass where a roll of sod had recently been laid. Jack noticed a pottery vase holding more daisies. A square black slab, just like Grandma's, was behind it.

"Go ahead. Take a look," said Grandpa. "It won't bite."

Jack looked up into the branches of the tree overhead. The leaves shivered and shimmied. He looked at the clouds scudding across the sky. He looked down over the town.

"Take your time, my little Wunderbar," said Grandpa. His hand on Jack's back was like someone breathing a secret against his skin.

# Chapter Eight

Jack stepped closer.

The white writing on the shiny black stone said:

*Neil (Noddy) Deacon 1953–2011*
*Beloved husband of Selena and father of Jeannie*
*Beloved grandfather of Jack Finch*

"That's you," said Jack. It didn't seem strange to be looking at his grandfather's headstone while he held his hand.

"So it is," said Grandpa.

They sat on the grass and looked at the headstone. Grandpa put his arm around Jack. Jack leaned against him. His grandfather felt as soft as a pillow and as cool as the breeze curling around Jack's head.

Together they listened to the birds in the tree above their heads. They watched the city traffic far below. The cars and buses looked as small as toys.

"I miss you," Jack said. How could he tell his grandfather he still felt all the missing he knew he would feel later?

"Of course you do," said Grandpa. "But just think of it. I get to spend my days close to Selena again. In a peaceful place. Me singing to the birds and the birds singing to me." He got up. Jack stood up too. "Now you know there's a quiet place you can come visit me anytime. That suit you, Tootsie Roll?"

"Mom said eight-year-olds are too young for hospitals, funeral homes and cemeteries."

"So I hear," said Grandpa. "But perhaps you can change her mind."

They stood together looking down at the graves. Then they walked back down the slope to the wrong bus.

"Besides," said Grandpa, "you're nine soon. Your birthday is just around the corner, if I recall."

In all the sadness and worry of Grandpa getting sick and then dying, Jack had forgotten all about his own birthday.

Thinking about it now, a bubble of happiness started to grow in his chest. He felt it melt the lump that had been there for days while his mother was visiting his grandfather in hospital. The lump had got bigger as she made plans at the funeral home. It had grown as hard as a stone when she left him home alone while she watched them bury his grandpa in the shiny brown coffin.

"My birthday is in two weeks," Jack said. He should start planning. Would he invite Katy over for cake? Maybe Mom would take them all out to a movie.

"I hope you didn't think I'd forgotten," said Grandpa, "just because I won't be there to help make a fuss of the birthday boy. I have something for you."

"What is it?" asked Jack.

"All will be revealed," said Grandpa. "In the fullness of time."

# Chapter Nine

Back in the bus, Grandpa Nod let Jack pull the knob to close the bus's doors. Jack sat on the long seat where he could watch his grandfather and the road at the same time.

This time, Grandpa stopped at the cemetery gates. He looked both ways before he pulled into traffic. At the bottom of the hill, he waited for the red light to change to green. Farther along, he hummed happily as he waited for the lady holding a Stop sign to let them go around a hole in the road.

He went the right way down one-way streets. He yielded to traffic when the sign told him to.

He stopped at a crosswalk while a man with a yellow Lab crossed the street. He stopped at another one while two ladies pushing shopping carts crossed.

But he didn't pull up to any bus stops. He just waved at the waiting passengers. He called out, "This is the wrong bus. Another will be along soon."

No one waved back.

Jack sat across from his grandfather and held on tight to the shiny pole. He studied Grandpa Nod's rosy cheeks. His eyes followed the creases down his face. He looked at the line across his forehead where his driver's cap had made a mark.

Over and over again Jack whispered the words on the gravestone at the top of the hill.

*"Beloved grandfather of Jack Finch."*

"Last stop," said Grandpa. He pulled up in front of Jack's school. "This is as far as this bus goes."

Jack could see three people waiting at the bus stop outside his school. But no one knocked on the door to get on. He felt the vibrations of the bus engine under his feet.

Jack knew it was time to get off. But something kept him in his seat, holding the silver pole. He studied his beloved grandfather in his blue uniform.

Grandpa Nod turned toward Jack. "Time's a-wasting, Milky Way."

"You said you had a present for me."

"So I did." Jack's grandpa rustled around in an untidy heap of papers on the dashboard. He slapped his forehead. "You have it already. In the side pocket of your backpack. You'll see."

Jack let go of the silver pole. He stood next to the driver's seat and leaned against his grandfather.

"I'm passing on my route schedules to you, Jelly Bean," said Grandpa Nod. "Everything I know that matters to anyone is in there."

"Everything?" asked Jack.

"Of every route I drove, for every day of the week."

Jack had been on all of Grandpa Nod's routes, at least once. Even six-year-olds and seven-year-olds are old enough to travel on buses alone if their grandfather is the driver.

"Thank you." He couldn't think of anything else to say.

His grandpa tapped the side of his backpack. "Keep them safe," he said. "You never know when you might need them. Now, give us a hug." He swung his legs around.

Jack hugged his grandpa. He felt warm and light in his arms.

"This is your stop, Oh Henry!" Grandpa pulled away and sat facing the steering wheel again. He pushed the knob. The door wheezed open. "Can't hold up this bus," he said.

Jack walked slowly down the stairs with his backpack tight on his shoulders.

Down on the sidewalk, he looked back up and waved. He couldn't see his grandfather's face. "Bye, Grandpa," said Jack.

He thought he heard the words "Goodbye, Jawbreaker," as the doors wheezed shut.

But he couldn't be sure.

Jack stood on the sidewalk and watched the bus merge with the traffic and drive off.

# Chapter Ten

"Have you been here the whole time?" asked Katy. She was at the front of the line at the bus stop. Her coat was falling off one shoulder and her face was pink. "I thought you would have left already," she said. "Were you afraid of taking the wrong bus?"

Jack looked into the traffic. There was no sign of his grandpa's bus now. He turned and looked the other way. The Number 26 was coming in their direction.

"I'm not worried about taking the wrong bus," Jack told Katy.

He thought of his grandpa's schedule safe in the pocket of his backpack.

"You going to sit next to me this time?" asked Katy.

"Sure," Jack said. "On one condition."

"What condition?"

"Quit telling everyone about my grandpa."

"That he died?" said Katy. "I was just trying to be helpful."

"I know. But don't do it. Okay? If I want anyone to know, I can tell them."

Katy shrugged. "Okay. Here's our bus."

Jack let Katy go ahead of him. He looked at the driver as he came up the stairs. It was a woman. A long ponytail hung over her shoulder. "Hi, Sweet Pea," she said. She checked his bus pass. "Had a long day at school?"

"Pretty long," said Jack. "But good."

He sat down next to Katy. She turned to look out the window.

Jack dug into the side pocket of his backpack. He found his grandpa's thick bundle of bus schedules

at the very bottom. They were held together by an elastic band.

He thought about the Number 13 bus Grandpa Nod drove on weekends. He drove it over the big bridge that soared over the Fraser River. And the Number 17. It was always full of noisy university students carrying takeaway coffees. He remembered the stops on the Number 31's route. It went right out to the ferry, where herons stood in the mud along the road.

He tucked the bus schedules back where he found them. He zipped up his backpack.

"The driver's new," Katy said. "I hope she knows where she's going."

Jack smiled. It didn't matter if the driver got lost. He would always have Grandpa Nod's bus schedules to help him find his way.

# Acknowledgments

Many thanks to editor Christi Howes, who helped *The Wrong Bus* safely reach its destination.

Lois Peterson discovered a new world when she started writing for kids of all ages. *The Wrong Bus* is her sixth book for Orca Book Publishers. For more information, visit www.loispeterson.blog.com.